Ali Baba
and the
Forty Thieves

Illustrated by Val Biro

Award Publications Limited

A long time ago, there lived a man called Ali Baba. He was a poor man. Each day he chopped wood in the forest and sold it at the market.

Ali Baba's cousin lived next door to him in a grand house. Cassim was lazy. He was wealthy and did not need to work hard like Ali Baba.

One day, as Ali Baba worked in the forest, some famous robbers – called the Forty Thieves – arrived. He quickly climbed up a tree to hide.

The thieves carried sacks filled with stolen gold and treasure. Their leader stood in front of a rock and said, "Open sesame!" A door then appeared in the rock!

Ali Baba watched the thieves carry their loot into the cave. When they left, he climbed down and said, "Open sesame!" The hidden door appeared in the rock again.

The secret cave was full of stolen treasure. Ali Baba took a sack of coins.

As he left he said, "Close, sesame!" to hide the door.

There were so many coins in the sack that Ali Baba could not count them all.

"I shall borrow a measuring scoop from Cassim," said his wife. Cassim's wife was suspicious. "What does Ali Baba need to measure? He's poor!"

Cassim's wife was crafty. She put sticky honey on the scoop.

When Ali Baba returned it, she saw a gold coin stuck to the bottom. Greedy Cassim demanded to know where Ali Baba had got the gold.

Ali Baba was a kind man and shared his secret with Cassim. But Cassim did not want to share.

He went to the cave to take all the treasure. But before he could leave, the thieves returned!

To save his own life Cassim told the thieves that Ali Baba had taken gold from the cave, and told them where he lived.

The leader of the thieves made a plan. He told his men to find forty large oil pots.

The Forty Thieves hid inside the pots, and the leader pretended to be an oil merchant.

He went to Ali Baba's house and asked for shelter for the night. He knew that Ali Baba was a good man and would not refuse to help.

Ali Baba invited him to stay. He offered him food and introduced him to his son, Ahmed.

But Ali Baba's maid, Morgiana, was suspicious.

After dinner, when the strange guest went outside, Morgiana secretly followed him. She heard him whisper to each jar, "Two knocks: attack tonight. Three knocks: wait till morning."

Morgiana ran to the chief of the City Guards and told him to bring his men to the bottom of the hill at sunrise.

"You will finally capture the Forty Thieves!" she said.

That night, the thieves' leader knocked twice on the jars: "Attack tonight."

But as soon as he had gone, clever Morgiana tapped three times on each jar: "Wait till morning."

Morgiana was secretly in love with Ali Baba's son.

She went to tell him what she had done. "Your father is in danger," she said. "Bring your friends at sunrise and we will catch the Forty Thieves!"

Ahmed did as Morgiana asked. At sunrise, he and his friends rolled the oil jars – with the thieves trapped inside – out onto the street...

...and down the steep hill. At the bottom the Forty Thieves were captured by the City Guards.

The leader of the thieves saw all this and realised he had been found out.

He took Ali Baba's donkeys and fled to the secret cave. He planned to run away with all the treasure.

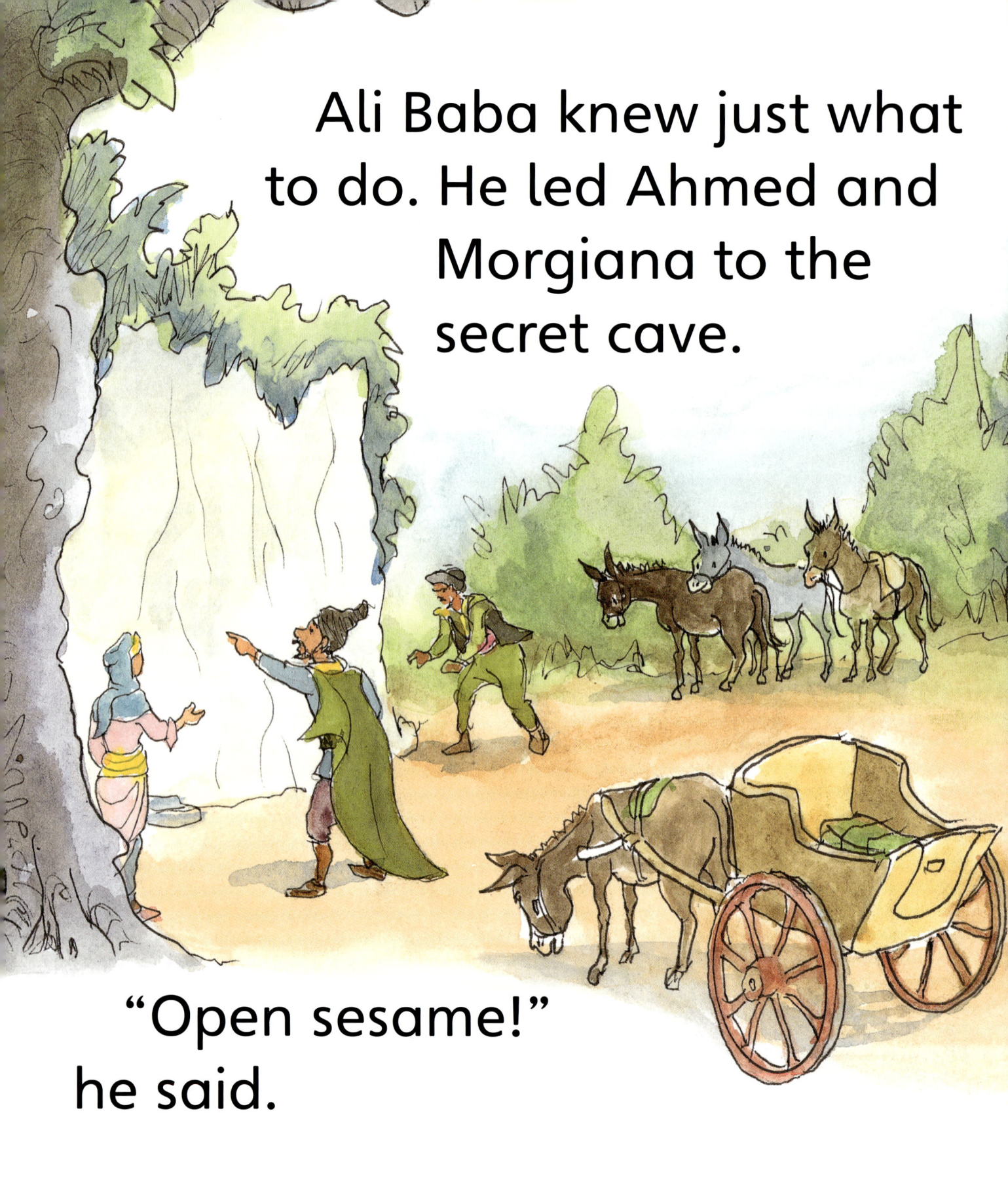

Ali Baba knew just what to do. He led Ahmed and Morgiana to the secret cave.

"Open sesame!" he said.

As the leader of the thieves ran from the cave, they jumped on him and tied him up. The City Guards rewarded them handsomely for their bravery.

Ali Baba was thankful to Morgiana for being so clever. And soon afterwards, Ahmed and Morgiana were married.